Dear Parent:
Your child's love of reading starts here!

Every child learns to read in a different way and at his or her own speed. Some go back and forth between reading levels and read favorite books again and again. Others read through each level in order. You can help your young reader improve and become more confident by encouraging his or her own interests and abilities. From books your child reads with you to the first books he or she reads alone, there are I Can Read Books for every stage of reading:

SHARED READING
Basic language, word repetition, and whimsical illustrations, ideal for sharing with your emergent reader

BEGINNING READING
Short sentences, familiar words, and simple concepts for children eager to read on their own

READING WITH HELP
Engaging stories, longer sentences, and language play for developing readers

READING ALONE
Complex plots, challenging vocabulary, and high-interest topics for the independent reader

ADVANCED READING
Short paragraphs, chapters, and exciting themes for the perfect bridge to chapter books

I Can Read Books have introduced children to the joy of reading since 1957. Featuring award-winning authors and illustrators and a fabulous cast of beloved characters, I Can Read Books set the standard for beginning readers.

A lifetime of discovery begins with the magical words **"I Can Read!"**

Visit www.icanread.com for information
on enriching your child's reading experience.

I Can Read!

READING
3
ALONE

The Just-So Woman

Story by Gary Blackwood
Pictures by Jane Manning

HarperCollinsPublishers

The Just-So Woman Text copyright © 2006 by Gary Blackwood Illustrations copyright © 2006 by Jane Manning All rights reserved. No part of this book may be used or reproduced in any manner whatsoever without written permission except in the case of brief quotations embodied in critical articles and reviews. Printed in the United States of America. For information address HarperCollins Children's Books, a division of HarperCollins Publishers, 1350 Avenue of the Americas, New York, NY 10019. www.harperchildrens.com

Library of Congress Cataloging-in-Publication Data

Blackwood, Gary L.

The just-so woman / story by Gary Blackwood ; pictures by Jane Manning.— 1st ed.

p.   cm. — (An I can read book)

Summary: When the Just-So Woman runs out of butter one day, she learns an important lesson from her neighbor, the Any-Way Man.

ISBN-10: 0-06-057727-4 (trade bdg.) — ISBN-13: 978-0-06-057727-8 (trade bdg.)

ISBN-10: 0-06-057728-2 (lib. bdg.) — ISBN-13: 978-0-06-057728-5 (lib. bdg.)

[1. Neighbors—Fiction.] I. Manning, Jane K., ill. II. Title. III. Series.

PZ7.B5338Ju 2006   2005028667

[E]—dc22   CIP

                                                                                                                              AC

1 2 3 4 5 6 7 8 9 10   ❖   First Edition

For my mother, who taught me to
milk a cow and to love books
—G.B.

To Auntie Jo, with love, from Goombie
—J.M.

Chapter One

The Just-So Woman gets out of bed
before the rooster crows.
She smoothes out the covers.
They do not need much smoothing,
for she does not toss and turn much.
Then she sweeps the floor.
It does not need much sweeping.
She does not drop many crumbs
or track in much dirt.

She feeds the cat.

She feeds the cows and chickens.

Then she fixes her breakfast.

She brews some mint tea.

She cuts a thick slice of bread.

But there is not a bit of butter.

"Oh, bother," says the Just-So Woman.

"Where has all the butter gone?

And what good is bread without it?

There is nothing to be done,

I suppose, but to make some more."

10

She takes her bucket to the barn,

where the milk cow waits.

She tries to sit on her stool

but sits, instead, in the straw.

"Oh, fiddle,"

says the Just-So Woman.

"The stool has a broken leg.

Well, there is nothing to be done

but to mend it, I suppose."

She hunts up her hatchet.

But it is too dull to please her.

"Oh, applesauce,"
says the Just-So Woman.
"I suppose there's nothing to be done
but to sharpen it."
She grinds it on the grindstone.

Then she takes a good, straight stick

and begins shaping it into a new leg.

The Any-Way Man strolls by

with his shabby-looking dog.

"Good morning," he says.

"What are you making there?"

"A new leg,"

says the Just-So Woman.

The Any-Way Man looks at her legs.

"Something wrong with the old ones?"

he asks.

The Just-So Woman sighs.

"It is for the milking stool," she says.

"Oh!" says the Any-Way Man.

"I just sit on a log, myself."

The Just-So Woman rolls her eyes.

"I am not surprised," she says softly.

"What's that?"

says the Any-Way Man.

"I said, I have got it to size," she says.
"If you will excuse me,
I must get on with the milking."
She does not like to be rude,
but the Any-Way Man can be trying,
with his devil-may-care ways.
She puts the new leg on the stool
and sits down to milk.

The warm milk streams

into the bucket

with a soothing sound.

The cat begs for a squirt of milk.

But that would be too messy.

As the Just-So Woman skims the cream
from the milk, she remembers
that she left the cow tied up.
She goes to untie the cow.
When she comes back,
the cat is licking
the cream spoon.

Chapter Two

The Just-So Woman

claps her hands at the cat.

"Bad cat! Now I must wash the spoon!"

But there is not a bit of soap.

"Oh, drat!" she says.

"There is nothing to be done

but to make some more."

She takes ashes from the stove

and runs spring water

through them to make lye.

She mixes the lye with lard
and boils them on the fire.
After the soap cools,
she washes the spoon with it.
Then she skims the cream.
She opens the top of the churn
to pour in the cream.
In the churn is a mouse nest.

"Oh, mercy!"

cries the Just-So Woman.

"What good is a cat

if mice build nests in the churn?"

The cat pays her no mind.

He is licking the spoon again.

"Well, there is nothing to be done
but to find them another home,"
she says.
She puts the tiny mice into her hat,
then washes out the churn.

Luckily she has lots of soap now.

As she churns the cream she sings,

"Come, butter, come.

Come, butter, come.

Johnny is waiting at the gate,

waiting for a honey cake.

Come, butter, come."

But of course no one is waiting.

It is only a churning song.

She feels the butter clump up.

She pours off the buttermilk.

But now she discovers

she is lacking something else—salt.

"Oh—" says the Just-So Woman.

She has run out of things to say

and has to start over.

"Oh, bother," she says.

"What good is butter

without a pinch of salt for flavor?"

"There is nothing to be done
but to try to borrow some."
And there is no one to borrow from
but the Any-Way Man.
She needs her hat for shade
from the hot midday sun,
but there is a mouse nest in it.
She has to make do with a scarf.

Chapter Three

The house of the Any-Way Man

is not like the Just-So Woman's.

It is not at all tidy.

But the Any-Way Man does have salt,

though the bag looks a bit dirty.

"I was about to fix some lunch,"

says the Any-Way Man.

"Would you care to join me?"

The Just-So Woman looks around

at the untidy kitchen

and at the dog, scratching its fleas.

"Oh, my, no," she says.
"It would not do to have lunch.
I have had no breakfast yet."
She thanks the Any-Way Man
and heads for home.

She feels a bit faint from the sun,

or from not eating.

She sits in her chair for a moment.

An hour later, or three,

she sits up and blinks her eyes.

"Oh, fiddle," she says.

"I must have dropped off.

It is not like me to be napping

when there are things to be done."

She works a pinch of salt
into the fresh butter.
Then she takes down the butter mold.
But there is a spot of white mold
on the wooden butter mold.

"Oh, crab apple sauce," she says.
"Even if I wash off the mold,
it will make the butter taste odd."
There is nothing to be done
but to borrow a butter mold.
And there is no one to ask
but the Any-Way Man.
She sighs and sets off again.

Chapter Four

The Any-Way Man scratches his head
and looks around his untidy house.
"Yes, there is sure to be a mold
somewhere around the place.
All I have to do is find it."
He begins moving this and that,
looking in here and under there.

He finds a butter knife.

He finds a bullet mold.

He even finds a bullet knife.

But not a butter mold.

The Just-So Woman sighs.
"Well, there is nothing to be done
but to use the butter as it is,
all plain and untidy."

But when she gets home,

every bit of butter is gone.

The cat is licking his whiskers.

"Bad cat!" says the Just-So Woman.

"Now what shall I eat on my bread?"

She sits in her chair,

feeling sad and worn out.

There comes a knock at the door,

but she is too tired to answer it.

"Come in," she says, "whoever it is."

It is the Any-Way Man.

"I found the butter mold," he says,

"and it is clean as a whistle,

for I almost never use it."

"Thank you,"

says the Just-So Woman.

"But now I have nothing to put in it.

The cat has eaten

every bit of the butter."

"I guess he did not care

whether it was molded or not,"

says the Any-Way Man.

"I guess sometimes it is best

just to take things as they are."

The Just-So Woman looks at him.

"That may be," she says.

"I was about to have some supper,

though I've had no breakfast or lunch.

Would you like to share with me?

I have no butter for the bread."

"I will tell you the truth,"
says the Any-Way Man.
"I do not use butter very much.
Mostly I dunk the bread in my tea—
that is, if I have any tea.
Have you ever tried it that way?"
The Just-So Woman smiles a little.
"No, I never have," she says.
"But you know what they say.

There is a first time
for everything."

Author's Note

One of the reasons I wrote *The Just-So Woman* was to give young readers a sense of what life was like on farms and homesteads before electricity, and before so much of the rural population moved to the suburbs and cities. Many of the things that we can just pick up at the store—including soap, bread, butter, and even bullets—used to have to be made at home. Farm wives who wanted their handiwork to be as attractive as possible packed their fresh butter—and sometimes their soap, too—into decorative wooden molds. The purpose of bullet molds—which were metal, not wood—was not to have attractive bullets but to be sure they were the right size for the rifle. After the melted lead hardened, the excess was trimmed off with a bullet knife.

Since I grew up in the 1950s, my life hasn't been quite as rustic as that of the Just-So Woman or the Any-Way Man. I've never made bullets or soap. But I have baked plenty of homemade bread, and sharpened an ax on a grindstone, and

milked a cow by hand (unlike the Just-So Woman, I always gave the cats a few squirts), and made my own butter—not in a churn, but by shaking the cream in a quart jar.